Holiday Lights and Cocoa Cookie Nights: A Sweet Later-in-Life Romcom Short Read

Interior Design by Mountain Heights Publishing

Author website: www.megeaston.com

ALSO BY MEG EASTON

Romancing the Spy romantic comedies

Spies Don't Fall for Their Asset

Spies Don't Fall for Their Rival

Spiced Chais and Secret Spies

Holiday Lights & Cocoa Cookie Nights

Spies Don't Fall for Their Neighbor (coming 2025)

How to Not Fall romantic comedies

How to Not Fall for the Guy Next Door

How to Not Fall for the Wrong Guy

How to Not Fall for Your Best Friend

How to Not Fall for Your Ex

A Mountain Springs Christmas

The Christmas Pact

The Christmas Bet

The Christmas Clause

Nestled Hollow Romance

Coming Home to the Top of Main Street

Second Chance on the Corner of Main Street

Christmas at the End of Main Street

More than Friends in the Middle of Main Street

Love Again at the Heart of Main Street

More than Enemies on the Bridge of Main Street

Love Started romances

It Started with a Sunset

It Started with a Note

It Started with a Glance

Silver Leaf Falls romance

Coming Home to Silver Leaf Falls

HOLIDAY LIGHTS & *Cocoa Cookie Nights*

MEG EASTON

CHAPTER 1

THE COVERT ART OF CHRISTMAS CHEER

Hammy

I glance at the group of us who've gathered at the Cipher Springs Public Library, toward the front doors, and then to the nearby stacks, casually looking for people trying to conceal their actions. Like the librarian who just innocently pushed her cart into the stacks furthest from the front desk while her secret love interest meanders toward the same area.

Why am I scanning the area? Because old intelligence operative instincts never really die, even though it's been a dozen years since I was last in the field and I'm living in a town where the most exciting things that happen are whatever antics the Barton teens are up to.

Those instincts made me a good operative. They're also the reason I've made it to age fifty-four.

Do I still need to wear this disguise that makes me look a

decade older? Probably not. I've been out of the field too long to be remembered. But I wear it everywhere except the office because covert instincts never really die, either. Especially since my current job is all about disguising operatives. And because the other club members wouldn't recognize me without it.

About twenty civilians have gathered for tonight's activity, which is impressive! When my physical therapy tech, Mackenzie, first told me over a year ago about her Outside the Bubble club, I came to one of the first meetings. There were only four of us.

For the record, I'm not here to get out of my bubble. My comfort zone is large enough that no activity we've done has made me step out of it. I'm here because living the bachelor life for so many years is rather lonely. I need people in my bubble. And the ones here are interesting.

Mackenzie welcomes us in a quiet voice. Then she says, "Are you ready for our special Christmassy Outside the Bubble club activity?"

Everyone enthusiastically whispers, "Yeah!" but not too loudly because we are in the library, and not only is there a *Quiet, please* sign five feet away, but there's also a librarian who could hold her own in a battle of severe expressions against the receptionist at the Clandestine Services Agency (and she's trained to scare people off).

Mackenzie grins at everyone's exuberant (yet muted) enthusiasm. "Okay, we've got six captains who are going to lead six service projects. You'll hear about your project from your captain." She puts the first two groups together, then says, "Our third captain is Reese, and the project is putting up Christmas lights. In that group, let's have...Hammy and Charlie."

So I get to team up with Charlie, one of my favorite people on earth, and Charlie's roommate, Reese, who always wears fun glasses and at least one honey, bee, or honeycomb-shaped piece of jewelry.

I grin as Charlie bounds over to me with her own grin. I've never had kids of my own, but my best friend, Rick, had six. He invited me into their lives from the start as "Uncle Abe." But since Rick died five years ago, I've been more of a stand-in dad for the youngest Lancaster, Charlie. She's a full-grown woman now, and an amazing tech operative and handler at the CSA.

"Did you bring enough warm clothes for working outside?" I ask her. Stand-in dad and all—it's my job to ask.

"Yep! Reese gave me advance warning about being outside. What about you? Will you be able to keep that balding head of yours warm?"

It's a good-natured ribbing. "Of course. 'Be prepared' has been my motto since I was a squeaky-voiced new Boy Scout." Plus, I have my own hair to keep me warm under the cap of balding hair I'm wearing.

It's fun to have people impressed at all I can do "at my age" (especially as a highly-trained ex-operative), but I wish that six years ago when I moved to Cipher Springs and decided on a disguise, I hadn't chosen to appear a decade older. At least I chose a name that's a nickname of mine. I am Abraham at work and Hammy in town, so if someone knows me by both—like Charlie—and accidentally calls me the wrong name, it's not suspicious.

Once the three of us are in Reese's compact SUV and are pulling out of the parking lot, Reese tells us about our assignment. "So, my parents got divorced about a year ago. Well, it was a long time coming before that—Oh, sorry!" she calls out to the car she just cut off. "I didn't see you!—but my dad officially moved out two days after Christmas. Anyway, my mom lives in a neighborhood where everyone has Christmas lights. It's her favorite thing, and she loves having them on her own house."

Reese takes a left turn like she doesn't know that one typically applies the brake a bit around corners, and we all lean to one side of the car.

"The small business who usually put up the lights closed. My mom's been super busy at work, and calling to schedule someone else slipped her mind. By the time she did, everyone was booked. Ooo—look at their lights!" Reese points at a house we're passing, and apparently, the steering wheel is connected to her eyes because we drift toward it. Until a car coming from the opposite direction honks, prompting her to get back into our lane.

"I would do it, but heights and I get along about as well as cats and vacuum cleaners. My mom won't ask my brother because he lives ninety minutes away and has an eight-month-old baby. But I know it really matters to her. So when Mackenzie announced she needed service project ideas, I suggested putting up my mom's lights because it's perfect! Plus, she's out of town for business so we can surprise her."

"That worked well," I say. What will also work well: arriving at Reese's mom's house in one piece. Reese has come to the last few Outside the Bubble activities, and from what I know of her, she's fun, thoughtful, and organized. I never guessed she was such a chaotic driver.

I only feel like my life is in the hands of a blindfolded carnival bumper car driver once more (when she slides on a patch of ice at an intersection) before she screeches to a stop in front of a good-looking home. It's fully dark outside, but from the porch and street lights, I can see the roof has several gables that will look nice with lights. There are about six inches of snow on the ground, so I can't see yard details, but I can tell there are shrubs near the home in one section and the rest is pretty clear.

Reese leads us inside her mom's garage, turns on the lights, shuts the door, and shows us where the boxes of Christmas lights are stored in the rafters. Three ladders are leaning against a wall, so I choose an A-frame one and set it up under the rafters.

I climb up, grab a box, and hand it down to Charlie. As I'm reaching for the second box, Reese says in a shaky voice, "Are you sure you're okay up there? You're up so high!"

I hand a second box to Charlie. "I'm fine. I've jumped out of airplanes dozens of times. Heights don't scare me." People in town don't know I've been a field operative, of course, but I don't hide that I've lived an adventurous life.

"Just… don't fall," Reese says. "I don't want you to get hurt."

I'm not going to get hurt. I may be in my fifties now, but I've been highly trained and I stay active. I grab the third box and hand it down.

"Yeah," Charlie adds, and I can hear the smile in her voice. "Because Mackenzie won't be happy if you need more physical therapy."

As I climb down, I say, "Mackenzie loves when I show up at her work." The injuries she treated were leftover from escapades in my earlier years—like an explosion that threw me through a third-story window before I landed on a car below, getting tangled in a helicopter's external ladder when a gust of wind caused the chopper to swerve and knock me into a pole, and from tumbling out of a moving train. Not from standing five feet up on a ladder.

We open the boxes to take stock of what we've got, and Charlie holds up a small container. "Are these all the clips we've got to attach the lights to the roof?"

We search again, and then Reese sighs. "I guess so. They'll have some at the hardware store, right? It's not far—I'll go buy more."

Charlie and I share a glance, and I see she's just as concerned about Reese's inattention to the road as I am. So she says, "I'll join you."

"Okay, then," Reese says, "it looks like we are going to the hardware store! Do you want to come, too, Hammy?"

I'd like to limit my time spent in a vehicle driven by Reese, and I'm more than ready to begin this project. I tell them I'll get started with the one box of clips we've got, give them a wave, and say, "Good luck, have fun, and don't die!" With Reese's driving, I mean the last part of the sentiment more than usual.

I'm at the top of a flat extension ladder I've leaned against the house, starting to hang the second string of lights, when a compact SUV pulls into the driveway. With Reese's driving, I shouldn't be surprised they're back so quickly. But I glance over and see that it's not Reese's vehicle.

Oh, no. That means it's likely her mom. This is Reese's surprise, and she isn't even here to see her mom's reaction. I need to hide so I don't spoil everything.

I haven't turned the Christmas lights on, so at least they aren't lighting me up. But if this woman hasn't already seen me, she will when she walks into her house. Instead of taking the time to climb down the ladder, I press my feet against its sides and walk it to the right so both the ladder and I can hide in the shadow of the streetlight where the house juts out.

When the vehicle's door opens, I hold perfectly still, barely breathing, since eyes are drawn to movement, hoping she won't look in my direction as she heads inside.

Then, I hear a woman say, "What do you think you're doing?"

Her voice is sharp, and I look down to see a woman traipsing through the snow toward me. She's wearing a pencil skirt and heels, keys in one hand, a leash in the other that's attached to a black and white Boston Terrier who's looking far too excited about walking across the snow. The woman is probably in her early fifties, thin, fit, and dressed nicely. And I see that my attempts to hide have made me appear very guilty. A mistake I know better than to make.

Before I can open my mouth to explain, she's almost to me, fists on her hips, eyes narrowed like I'm a thief in the night, and says, "Why are you climbing to my roof?"

Her puppy, sensing either tension or excitement, seems determined to join the action and races forward, yanking the leash from the woman's hand. It's not a big dog but it's an enthusiastic one, and it's headed straight for my ladder.

The string of lights I've just started putting up is wrapped once around my arm so the weight of the part still coiled on the snow below won't pull the other end from the two clips I've already secured it in. I attempt to get free of the lights so I can better respond to the threat to remaining in my precarious position that's coming at me in the form of a black-and-white powerhouse fur ball, but the puppy pounces into my ladder too quickly.

Before I know it, my ladder is wobbling, the woman is yelling, "Spark, no," and the dog is grabbing the string of lights, which pulls my arm and makes me completely lose my balance.

I fall onto the shrubs below that cushion me a bit before I tumble off them and onto the snow, right on top of the Christmas lights, the fall knocking the air out of me. The other end of the lights breaks free from the two clips at the edge of the roof, and the string trails behind, landing on top of me.

Okay, falling from ten feet up a ladder as a fifty-four-year-old is definitely different from falling as a twenty-something.

The woman shrieks as the puppy dives into the mess of lights, dancing all over me and the lights. It barks like it caught a fugitive. I'm on my back in the snow and tangled in the lights, the Boston Terrier is now tangled in the lights, and the woman—who must feel the need to either stop the Grinch here to steal Christmas or join the fray to save her dog—has slipped onto her rear and is also tangled in the lights.

I push up onto my elbows. The woman and I are trying to get free from the strings of lights but the puppy is soaking in every bit of fun from this game of lights-and-new-people, and the only thing we're accomplishing is to make the lights tighten around us. The leash that's tangled in the mix isn't helping, either.

The dog must decide that "new people to play with" is the better part of the game, and it gets right on top of my chest to lick my entire face.

The woman is searching her coat pockets. "Where's my phone? I'm calling the police." I'm trying to lift the pup off me long enough to sit and get free of the lights, but it keeps jumping back onto me like I'm the best part of this new game. The woman stops trying to find her phone and says, "Hey,

Siri. Call nine-one-one on speaker." Then she says to her dog, "Spark! Stop. Licking. The. Burglar!"

"I'm not a burglar!" I say as a muffled-in-a-coat-pocket voice says, "Nine-one-one, what's your emergency?"

Hearing the operator's voice helps the woman find her phone and she pulls it from a pocket. "I'm trapped in front of my house with a burglar! Send help quickly!" She tries to pull the puppy off me but the strands of lights hold her back. She gives the 9-1-1 operator her address, the dispatcher says they have an officer nearby, and then the woman narrows her eyes at me. "Nice try, but just saying you aren't a burglar isn't getting you out of this. I wasn't born yesterday."

I can tell she's got a good amount of adrenaline coursing through her by her dilated pupils, fast breathing, and tense muscles. So I say, *"I'm not the Grinch,"* in a calm voice, hoping a different tone and phrasing will work better—a trick I learned in the field. "I'm Santa's elf."

This does get her to stop fighting against the lights long enough to look at me and say, "You're *what*?"

"I'm not here to steal Christmas—I'm here to…bring Christmas cheer." I give her a sheepish grin, hoping she buys my story, and Spark puts its own exclamation mark on my declaration by giving me a long lick up my cheek.

She studies me in the glow of the porch light like she's judging my trustworthiness. I watch her emotions change as her eyes shift from the tangled mess of lights we're in to the ladder that has fallen, to the one string of lights running along her roof I already installed. Since they're not on, they're difficult to see in the dim light unless you're really looking. Then, she gasps.

I'm also noticing how beautiful that face of hers is. Her blond and whitish-gray hair is pulled into a loose bun, and I realize how beautiful it is, too. Now that she seems to accept I'm not a thief, I can tell that she's viewing me differently, too. There's a charge of electricity between us that surprises and thrills me. Some sparks are definitely flying, and I'm not referring to the dog.

Then, suddenly, instead of the woman's hair being bathed in the warm glow of the porch light, it's lit with flashing blue and red. The 9-1-1 operator wasn't kidding when she said they had someone nearby.

CHAPTER 2

LIGHTING UP THE NEIGHBORHOOD

Annette

Now that my rush of alarm is subsiding, I can see in the darkness there have been clues all around me that this man is putting up Christmas lights—he wasn't sneaking onto my roof, even though that's exactly what it looked like.

The police officer parked out front is halfway across the lawn to us, the lights on his car still flashing, when Reese's car skids to a stop just behind his. That daughter of mine is going to pop another tire if she keeps coming at curbs so fast.

She leaps out and races across the lawn, passing the officer, calling out, "Mom! Are you okay? Is someone hurt?" When she reaches us, she adds, "Hammy, I told you not to fall off the ladder! Mom, you weren't up the ladder, too, were you?"

Spark barks, happy as ever.

"You know this man?" I ask her.

She nods. "This is Hammy from Outside the Bubble Club."

Reese's roommate, Charlie, catches up a second later. She crouches beside the man, putting an arm around his shoulders. "And he's my honorary dad."

"We're doing service projects," Reese says, "and we decided to put up your lights because I know how important it is to you."

"For the record," the man tangled with me says as he motions with arms strewn in lights toward the flashing red and blue on my house, "those are not the lights I was trying to bring to the season."

The nice thing about being on this earth for a little over five decades is that you no longer get as easily embarrassed as you did in your younger years. But apparently, accusing a man who's trying to help of being a thief, your dog knocking him off his ladder, falling onto your rear, and getting tangled in a mess of lights—while wearing a pencil skirt, of all things —is enough to do it. My face is probably as red as Santa's suit. Hopefully, everyone assumes it's from the cold.

Reese begins untangling the Christmas lights trapping me as I apologize to Hammy. By the time Reese offers a hand to pull me to my feet, I've said "I'm sorry" using about every phrase possible. It's a bit of a rambling blur, but I might've even said, "My bad," and "Oopsie-Daisy," two phrases I'm sure I've never said in my life.

I pick up Spark and cradle her to my chest. Once my dog and I are no longer tangled with him, Hammy has no problem at all hopping to his feet.

"So..." a voice behind me says, "I take it everything is okay?"

I whirl around to face the officer, who I somehow completely forgot about. Even with his flashing lights bouncing off my house, my neighbors' houses, and the snow that covers everything. I apologize to him, too.

Once the officer is pulling away, I say, "Give me a minute to change," then I grab my suitcase and my puppy and head into my house. As soon I shut the door behind me, I close my eyes and take in a slow breath. I can't believe I thought that man was breaking into my house! I blame it on the fact that I was just on a full flight, seated between a kid watching *Home Alone* and a man watching *Die Hard*.

I change into warmer clothes and snow boots and head back out to join the awkward situation. I stand at the base of Hammy's ladder and feed the string of lights up to him as Charlie untangles the mess we made by getting trapped in them. Reese is handing clips up to Hammy and frequently voicing her worries that he might fall again.

I have to admit I'm glad I took the earlier flight home and got assigned this task because I have a great view of Hammy's backside. And it's a really nice backside. Especially for someone his age. Not that I know how old he is. By his face and hair, I'm guessing he's in his sixties. Maybe even sixty-five. But his physique is of someone closer to my age who likes to stay fit and active.

It hits me that this might be the first time I've checked out a man's backside since Bryce. Reese will be so proud! She's been trying to nudge me toward dating again.

And there's more to check out than just Hammy's looks—his movements are mesmerizing. Each time he repositions the ladder, he places it so perfectly that it never needs adjusting. I've never heard someone climb up and down a ladder so silently before. And he has such incredible balance that he never holds onto the ladder or house—he just attaches clips and lights quickly and seamlessly.

He's one capable man. And so willing to help. It's been a long time since I've had that in my life. "So, Hammy," I ask. "How did you get so good at working atop a ladder?" Maybe he has a career in home construction.

He twists to look at me and says with a wink, "Oh, that's from my covert infiltration training as a top-secret government spy."

I can't help it—I laugh heartily. I'm glad he's already viewing my accusing him of thievery through the lens of humor. I appreciate that.

"What do you do for a living?" he asks.

"I work at a promotional products company."

"She doesn't just work there," Reese says, "she's an executive."

Hammy's eyebrows rise. "Impressive."

I shrug as I work a minor tangle out of the lights. "It's a byproduct of working at the same company for over a decade." Well, that, and working my tail off.

"Is your company *Merchify Your Brand*?"

This time, my eyebrows shoot up in surprise. "You know us? Usually, people don't." I tap a finger on my lips. "Let me guess. You know because of the secret spy thing."

An expression flashes on Hammy's face that's hard to read. "Yes. As a spy, I've often found that promotional sunglasses are great for going undercover at beach resorts, especially when they're comically large ones. Espionage and sunbathing overlap more than you'd think. Oh, and those glow-in-the-dark key chains are surprisingly handy for marking covert drop locations at night."

"And let me guess. You get the branded magnets for securing mission blueprints to the fridge in the spy lounge?"

"I didn't realize our secret was out. Did you also know that we use custom mouse pads and spy logo mugs as consolation prizes for operatives who get stuck with desk duty?"

"I *didn't*. But I heard you use the branded lip balm before tense negotiations because chapped lips—"

"—are the real enemy," we both say at the same time. I can't help laughing. Hammy is so fun to talk to. "We've been missing out on so many customers by not marketing to spy agencies! I'll have to talk to our sales department."

"You might double your profits."

Hammy and I smile at each other for a moment before he climbs down. As he's moving the ladder to the next area, he says, "Actually, I work for a business solutions company where I do a lot of graphic design and corporate branding. I create the images, and I recommend our clients order their promotional products from your company."

A smile spreads across my face. I've worked tirelessly at Merchify Your Brand. Meeting someone who's been recommending us to their clients is like spotting a unicorn in the wild.

Mostly because of Hammy's efficiency, we finish much too soon. Reese sends us to the sidewalk in front of my house, does a dramatic countdown, and then turns on the holiday lights. We all clap and cheer. I even get a little teary-eyed. Lights are one of my favorite things about Christmas, and I didn't think I'd get to see them on my house this year.

Not only do I want to thank everyone for making my house look so festive and beautiful but I want to talk more with Hammy, so I invite everyone in for hot chocolate. I get Spark food and water first since she's been so patient. As I'm opening my cupboards and fridge to get ingredients, I say, "I have a recipe I made when my kids got together with friends to sled down Doomslide Summit."

"I loved that place," Reese says wistfully before adding a much more robust, "I survived Doomslide!" as she throws her fist into the air.

I loved the place, too, because of how much happiness it brought my kiddos. I find the recipe to make sure I haven't forgotten anything over the years. Whew! I'm not missing any ingredients.

As I'm pouring milk into the pot, Reese comes over and I say, "I can't believe you set this all up. Thank you."

"I can't believe you came home early." She pops a chocolate chip into her mouth.

"Today would've been less embarrassing if I'd kept my original flight, that's for sure."

Reese grins. "Well, you've been saying you want more excitement in your life."

"Not in the form of me accusing 'Santa's Elf' of being a Grinch!" Although, chatting with Hammy did start to fill my empty need-for-excitement bucket.

"You don't have enough excitement in your life?" Hammy asks.

I shrug. "I haven't done anything simply for fun in so long. Between running a business and running a family, I didn't have anything left for fun."

"We should change that," Hammy says. "How about the two of us sled down Doomslide Summit tomorrow night? It's supposed to snow in the morning, so there'll be fresh stuff waiting for us. We'll pack the most fun into one night that's possible."

A smile spreads across my face. I've never wanted to date

just for entertainment. But going on a date with Hammy for pure enjoyment is something I can't pass up. *"The most amount of fun possible?* Obviously, I have to say yes."

Hammy smiles. "It's a date, then."

I turn to stir the hot cocoa and smile. A date. I've got myself *a date.*

CHAPTER 3

FUN ANNETTE, MEET ADVENTURE HAMMY

Hammy

The snowfall stopped early this afternoon. The plows have cleared the roads, the skies are clear, and the moon and stars are lighting the newly fallen snow. The perfect conditions for a first date. I haven't stopped thinking about it all day.

I glance at Annette, who I picked up moments ago. Not only is she dressed in warm enough gear that we won't have to stop because of the cold, but she has a grin on her face like she's legitimately excited.

"It took some searching to find where Doomslide Summit is," I say. "Did you know it's not an officially named hill?"

Annette laughs. It's not a chuckle and it's not a hearty laugh. It's a musical thing, and it's a beautiful sound. "Good thing you have those spy skills to help you out."

I can't believe I'd said I gained skills by training as a spy.

First, I was an intelligence operative. Second, that's a secret I guard fiercely, not something I joke about. I'd flinched the moment I said it yesterday and was hoping she'd forget about it. But here we are.

I nod. "Otherwise, I couldn't have checked it out already to gauge whether I'm manly enough to brave it."

She laughs a bit more this time. "Did you decide that you are?"

I shrug, even though this hill is no match for me. Not long ago, I sped down an Olympic luge track on my back with a thin fiberglass and steel sled between me and the track. And the track had parabolic curves and hairpin bends. But I'm not here to brag or sound like I'm bragging. So I say, "I don't know. It sounds pretty intense."

I haven't dated for a while, but I dated a lot in my younger years. As a field operative, I never allowed any relationship to move beyond casual because I didn't think my job and a serious relationship could coexist. After leaving the field for the role of Director of Covert Identity and Disguise, I could've settled down and had a real relationship, but I never found anyone who really grabbed me. Until now. Annette has grabbed hold of me firmly and I can't stop thinking about her.

"Please," Annette says. "I watched you hang lights like it was a Sunday stroll."

"Ahh, but they didn't train us in snow tubing." I did do an *Escape and evasion techniques using natural terrain* course and part of that was descending uneven mountainous areas, but I can honestly say we didn't get "snow tubing" training.

"So you're saying this could be more dangerous than a covert operation?" she asks.

"Maybe. If you hear me shout 'abort,' you'll know." I'll

admit I do enjoy joking with her about the spy thing even if it makes me flinch.

I park near the top of the hill and pull the inflated snow tubes out of the back of my crossover. As we walk to the hill, I ask, "So, when was the last time you did this?"

"Oh, wow. Um…" Annette thinks for a moment. "Probably when Reese was still too young to sled by herself. She was five the first time she braved it alone, so the winter before that."

"A couple of decades, then?"

"Sounds about right."

"That's too long ago," I hand her a tube. "I'm glad we're going to remedy that."

The hill is long and decently high. We're probably going to get some good speed going down. I can see why it's a favorite sledding spot—there is plenty of flat, open field at the end of the hill. Well, except for one section toward the bottom where it looks like some kids piled up snow to make a ramp.

I drop our tubes, then spot a sturdy stick a couple of feet long and pick it up before we both get situated on our tubes. They have handles on the sides, and we grasp the ones on the outsides, but I reach across to grab hold of her inside handle and she grabs hold of mine, linking us together.

"Ready?" I ask.

She nods, but I can see she's a bit nervous.

"Any tips you'd like to share before we take off?" I ask. "You know, besides 'Close your eyes and hope for the best.'"

"I recommend keeping them open until we're aimed in the right direction. Unless you want to risk veering toward that ramp."

"Solid advice. Okay, to both of us—good luck, have fun,

and don't die!" I use the stick like an oar to nudge us toward the slope. Then, I drop it and grab onto my handle.

We pick up speed quickly. We're both making sounds like a rallying cry mixed with pure exhilaration and for Annette, occasionally a scream. Our tubes start to turn, and then we're going down backward before eventually spinning to face the direction we started. By the time we slow at the base, we're both laughing.

"That was such a rush!" Annette says as we get off our tubes. "I'd forgotten how fun this is!"

Her cheeks are flushed—although that could be windburn from our descent—and her eyes are alive with excitement.

As we head toward the hill, hauling our tubes and still breathing heavily from the adrenaline, she asks, "So, is this normal for you?"

I glance at her. "Snow tubing?"

She shrugs. "Adventurous things in general."

"I…" I pause, carefully choosing my words, "have been known to participate in extreme sports now and then." I try to take in every facet of emotion on her face. If I have to guess, I'd say her expression is part impressed, part longing, and something else I'm unsure of.

"Do you have kids?" she asks. "I mean, beyond an honorary daughter."

"Not unless you count the other Lancaster kids. I was their honorary uncle until their dad, Rick, passed away five years ago, and now I'm an occasional stand-in dad for them, too. But no, I never married. I traveled so much—sometimes without advance notice—that I didn't think a relationship could work."

"I wouldn't have guessed that graphic design and branding would require so much time away from the office."

"I don't only do it in-house, like many in my profession. And our clients tend to be…a bit demanding."

"Do you still travel a lot?"

"Nah. I leave that for the younger ones. How about you?"

She turns her focus to Doomslide Summit as we get to the more uphill part. "Not too much. Five or six times per year." She winks. "The rest I leave for the younger ones."

We're mostly up the very long hill when Annette looks over the snowy landscape lit by the nearly full moon. "I thought by the time I was an empty nester, I'd be celebrating the holidays somewhere warm. On a beach, a coconut drink in my hand, soaking in the sun and watching the waves. Not clinging to an inflatable tube, praying for mercy from a hill named 'Doomslide.'"

"Eh, the beach is overrated—it's hot, sand gets everywhere, and it's not easy to wash off."

"Snow might wash off easily, but you end the day with soaking wet everything."

"True," I say. "But if you get injured, you don't even need an ice pack. You can just flop down in the snow."

Annette laughs. "Making snow angels and healing bruises in one fell swoop."

"Another reason why snow wins in a match against the beach."

We finally make it to the top of the hill. "Speaking of winning a match…" Annette says as she takes off running toward the middle. "You better hurry, because this time, we are racing each other down!"

We leap onto our tubes from a run and the momentum sends us down the hill. I jumped onto mine from an angle, so now I'm spinning. When I face forward again, I see I'm headed straight toward the piled-up snow that's making a ramp.

When I hit the jump, it sends me and my tube airborne. I'm guessing I'm a dozen feet in the air, and I whoop the entire time. I don't land flat, so I'm sent tumbling across the snow. I'm laughing, though, so when Annette's face appears over me, I see that she's not concerned.

"Were you showing off your acrobatic skills, or are you injured and the rolling is to get the full-body ice pack?"

I wink. "Maybe a bit of both."

By the time we make it to the top of the hill a third time, Annette has decided that she wants to go off the jump, too. She gets lined up to head straight toward it, and I give her tube a little nudge over the edge before hopping onto my own and cheering for her the whole way down.

She hits the ramp perfectly. Other than some mid-air feet flailing and a half-exhilarated, half-terrified squeal, she does it so much more gracefully than I did.

When Doomslide Summit tires us out and we start getting cold, I drive us to a nearby outdoor skating rink solely for the big fire they have every night, and we take a seat on a bench near it to warm our toes. I open my bag and pull out two mugs and the spiced apple cider that's been staying warm in a thermos. I fill both mugs and hand one to Annette.

She removes her gloves and wraps her hands around the mug, holding it to her nose, closing her eyes, and breathing in the scent. I love that she enjoys small things like that.

I take out a container of cookies, open it, and hand her one. "This is to warm your taste buds." I grab one, too, and take a bite as she does. She's savoring the bite, and I can tell the moment that she feels the subtle heat of the cookie.

Her eyebrows rise, and as soon as she swallows, she says, "Spicy cookies?"

I nod. "'Hot Cocoa Cookies.' And the 'hot' isn't because they're fresh out of the oven."

"They're delicious! Did you make these?"

I shake my head. "I occasionally do, but I didn't make these. This was my favorite cookie as a kid. One day at work, I described them to Charlie and said I wished I could find them somewhere. She has the superpower of discovering the best place to go for things like baked goods.

"The next day, she comes into work with a box in her hands, beaming. She'd found these—the exact cookie of my childhood. I picked them up on my way to your house."

As we're eating the cookies and drinking the cider, Annette leans into me. It's only a bit, but it confirms I'm not the only one feeling a connection.

When Annette finishes her second cookie, she puts her mug on the bench beside her, brushes off her hands, and then swings one leg over the bench so she's facing me. I do the same to face her.

"So, Hammy, speaking of this season of life turning out differently than we guessed, did you ever expect to get tangled in Christmas lights with a woman one night, then tube down a snowy hill with her the next?"

I didn't even think to dream about that or I would have. "No," I say with a sly smile, "but now I know what I want my retirement plan to be."

Something crosses Annette's face that I can't interpret. Uncertainty, maybe?

She shakes her head. "I'm not thinking about retirement—I'm still trying to figure out what happened to Fun Annette.

She left around age thirty-two and hasn't been seen since. I think she might be in witness protection."

"Fun Annette isn't gone. She just went on a covert mission for a bit." And this time, it's me bringing up operatives. It's almost like I want Annette to know.

"And now it's time for me to 'come in from the cold'? That's what they call it, right?"

I chuckle. "I think that's for operatives who've gone rogue."

"Maybe Fun Annette *did* go rogue, and she's out there making questionable decisions and hiding from Responsibility Annette."

"I've only ever seen Fun Annette. Well, and *Stop, Thief!* Annette. What makes you feel like you lost her?"

"That's not a conversation topic for a first date."

"Are you worried it'd scare me off? I mean, in the past—" I glance at my watch—"twenty-eight hours, I've been pulled off a ladder by a protective canine, tangled in lights, accused of being a thief, faced Doomslide Summit, and braved going airborne off a ramp made by children, and I'm not scared yet."

Annette laughs. "Fair enough. Okay. Well, I was married for twenty-seven years, but I didn't exactly have a partner. In the beginning, it was easy to let Fun drive our lives. Then, we had a child, so Responsibility took the wheel and Fun was pushed to the passenger's seat. Bryce didn't like that, so he decided to get in his own car so Fun could still drive instead of staying in the family car with us.

"Then we had a second child, and as she grew, more and more responsibilities piled in—school, homework, sports, making healthy meals, doctor visits, never-ending laundry, play dates, music lessons, making sure soccer cleats still fit, and science fair projects got completed—and Fun got pushed to the back seat. Then to the trunk. At some point, without even noticing it happened, it fell right out the back."

Annette puts a hand on her forehead before using it to brush her hair away. "It's not like I hated any of those responsibilities. Well, maybe laundry. And I can't blame everything on Bryce—that's not fair. I mean, who knows? Maybe I'd be exactly where I am either way. I guess that's not the point. It's that now I *can* let Fun Annette take the wheel but I don't know how to entice her back."

I study her for a moment. "I've got an idea." I pull out my phone to look up the city's list of activities for the holidays. And then my phone starts to ring. Not the one in my hand, but the one in my coat pocket. There's an instant shift in energy between us the moment she realizes I have a second phone.

"I am so sorry. This is work. Can you give me a minute?"

I walk a dozen feet away as I answer. It's my assistant, Soren. He's at the office, working late. The 3D printer is out of ink and he can't find any. As I'm explaining where it is, I look at Annette. If her ex-husband had been letting Fun drive, there were probably times when she felt she couldn't trust him. Maybe he even had his own second phone. It isn't hard to guess that she likely has trust issues.

And then there's me. I've spent most of my life wearing disguises and pretending to be different people. I've been pretending to be Hammy for the past six years. Like I'm any better.

Soren finds the ink. I hang up, slide the phone into my pocket, and head back to the bench by the fire where Annette is waiting.

To keep things light, I say, "Well, Fun Annette has definitely come in from the cold tonight. I'd say that the best way to keep her around is to keep inviting her back for more 'missions.'"

"Oh, yeah?"

I nod, thinking I shouldn't ask her on another date but desperately wanting to. "Tonight was part one of her re-orientation. The Lancaster family's Secret Santa night is a lot of fun, and it's this weekend. What do you say to going with me? We can entice Fun Annette to stick around."

She smiles. "I think I'd like that."

CHAPTER 4

ALL I WANT FOR CHRISTMAS IS CLUES

Annette

I walk with Hammy to the corner of Keyhaven Park to meet the Lancaster family before heading into the holiday market and festival. The air is crisp and fresh and although it's cold, it's not bitingly so. The sun has set, but the entire park is well-lit.

I used to bring my kids to this event. There are vendor booths, a stage where local groups sing Christmas songs, and Santa's Workshop and Village. We loved it all. This event always draws lots of families.

I'll admit I was a little thrown a couple of nights ago when Hammy pulled out a second cell phone, probably because of everything with Bryce. I decided not to freak out, especially because Hammy and I had so much fun! I didn't want the night to end. He must not have, either, because we sat by the fire, talking, until they kicked us out.

I spot five people waiting at the park's corner. A woman who's about my age and looks like she could take charge of any situation is talking to a younger couple whose backs are to us. A tall man with broad, beefy shoulders stands with a blond, athletic woman. Hammy waves, but they don't react. As if they didn't realize he was waving at them.

As we get closer, Hammy says, "Hi, everyone," and the couple whose backs are to us turn around, and their faces light up in recognition.

"Hammy!" the woman says as she hugs him. "I'm so glad you could come!" She's probably in her mid-twenties and has wavy brown hair.

"I wouldn't miss this event for anything," Hammy says. Then he introduces me to the woman, Mackenzie, who was his physical therapy tech. Her fiancé, Jace, is at her side, the beefy man is Jace's brother, Ledger, the athletic blonde is his girlfriend, Zoe, who apparently is meeting Hammy for the first time, and the woman my age is Evelyn. She's the matriarch.

More join us, including Charlie, and I'm introduced to three more brothers—Emerson, Blake, and Miles—and a toddler named Heidi. They're a lovely family. I can see why Hammy is so fond of them.

But except for Charlie, as each of the others neared, they seemed to initially not recognize Hammy. Yet as they interact, it's obvious that they all know him very well. I don't know what to think about it.

I'm not the only one new to this activity—Zoe is, too—so Evelyn explains the rules. We'll pair up with each other to find a child to buy a gift for. We can't communicate with the child or their family, so we have to see what draws their attention before buying their gift. Then we wrap it and deliver it to them in a way that makes them believe they got it from Santa.

"Giving the gift can be as simple as leaving it in the child's path with their name on it," Evelyn says, "or it can be as elaborate as you like. As long as it happens within the borders of the park and you make it back here before time's up."

Miles sighs. "I miss the good ole days when we could deliver it to the child's home."

"I don't miss my broken leg," Emerson says.

"You've got to admit, though," Jace says, "that those 'reindeer hoof' prints we left in the snow on their roof were pretty awesome."

Emerson nods. "But the body print of me sliding off the roof and onto their inflatable Santa hat-wearing penguin wasn't."

"Oh!" Ledger says. "Remember that catapult we used once to send the gift right to the kid's front door?"

Several of the Lancaster siblings look upward, wistfully.

Not Blake, though. He says, "If only it hadn't terrified the homeowners."

Ledger shakes his head. "Only for a second. Once they saw the gift, they knew they weren't under attack."

"It took more than a second for the bomb squad to verify that the gift was not, in fact, an explosive."

Hammy leans in close. "We didn't always have a time or location limit. Things got a little too…creative and had to be reined in a bit."

I chuckle. "I can see that."

"Oh," Emerson says, "but Abe—*Hammy's* drone that you two altered to look like Santa's sleigh—you've got to admit that was pretty great."

Hammy grins at Charlie. "If only the gift had fallen into the child's waiting arms as we'd planned."

"Yeah," Charlie says, "we should've chosen a less-breakable gift."

I'm not entirely sure what to think of all this, but I do love the excitement in the air. I lean into Hammy. "Are things always this thrilling around you?"

"Nah—sometimes I like staying home for cocoa cookie nights."

Okay, that sounds pretty great, too.

"Are we going to stand around all night, reminiscing," Evelyn asks, "or are we going to go be Secret Santas? We've got seventy-five minutes, starting…Now."

Everyone looks at their watches simultaneously. Then, as we head away in pairs, Hammy calls back to the group, "Good luck, have fun, don't die!"

I grab his arm. "Wait. Everyone doesn't still get super crazy with it, do they?"

Hammy looks at me, confused. "Oh, because of the 'don't die'? That's just something I started saying as a kid whenever my dad left on some crazy adventure. It still reminds me of him every time I say it."

I smile. Okay, that's really sweet, actually. "Should we go to Santa's Workshop or village to find a child?"

Hammy shakes his head. "That's what Jace and I thought the first time we did this, back when he was little and we were paired up. We found lots of kids, sure, but where we really get clues about what they want is in the holiday market."

We spot Ledger and Miles in the first aisle of vendors, so we go down another and pretend to look at treats, handmade crafts, and gifts while surreptitiously keeping an eye out for a child in need of a gift.

As we go from booth to booth, several people say "Hi" to Hammy and are happy to see him. It doesn't surprise me—he's a friendly guy. What's still surprising me, though, is how the Lancasters reacted to seeing Hammy. They're the people who know him best. And if I understand correctly, he works with most of them daily. Why did they act like they didn't recognize him?

My skepticism aside, I love being here with Hammy. We look at Christmas items for sale, try on Santa hats, sample peppermint bark and spiced nuts, and debate which Christmas song is the best. After about ten minutes, I ask, "Did you spot any kids we should choose?"

Hammy is looking at a snow globe with a small town scene. He nods toward a high-energy boy with tousled hair who's about six and is currently turning the cranks on a mechanical Santa display, trying to understand how it works. "The mini mechanic over there, or the budding artist across the aisle and two booths back. What about you?"

I turn to see the same little girl I'd noticed. She's probably seven, is quiet and observant, drawn to anything creative, and gazes at art half mesmerized, half longing. "I noticed the same two, actually."

Hammy smiles. "Who do you think we should pick?"

I look at both kids again while pretending to admire a carved wooden reindeer. "The girl's pants are too short, her shoes are worn, and her coat's too big. I know what it's like to have a budget that won't stretch far enough for anything that isn't an absolute necessity."

"And did you see the way she carefully touched the display of markers in that art supply booth?" Hammy shakes his head. "I couldn't hear as she told her mom about them, but I saw the mom's lips. She said they were too expensive, but she can tell Santa about them before they leave."

"We have to get them for her," I say.

Hammy gives me the sweetest look. Like he adores me. I don't remember the last time a man looked at me in adoration. "Let's do it."

We hurry to the art supply booth and buy the markers, a sketch pad with big sheets of paper, sketching pencils and erasers, some colored pencils, a set of watercolor paints and paint brushes, some glitter gel pens, and an art supply case.

Then we take it to a gift wrapping station and choose some Christmas paper with paint splatters. As the woman in the booth wraps the present, we spot the girl standing by her mom, watching a man carve a five-foot-tall chunk of ice with a chainsaw, turning it into a nutcracker soldier.

I look at Hammy. "What if we do a scavenger hunt as a way to give the girl her gift? Since she's going to see Santa at the end, we can have him tell her that he's got a present for her and give her the first clue."

"That's perfect!"

We are grinning at each other like we're a couple of kids. We buy four cards from the present wrapping station that have the same splattered paint theme, and then we work on a plan.

Working with Hammy is a pretty amazing thing. We worked together when putting up the lights, tubing down the hill, and tonight, being Secret Santas. I remember this feeling—I felt it with Bryce when we first got married, then never again. I'd forgotten how incredible it is to work toward the same goals with someone. I could easily become addicted to the feeling. And addicted to spending time with

Hammy. And feeling things I haven't felt in a gazillion years.

We spot the girl in Santa's Workshop creating a snowflake by gluing wooden craft sticks together. Most of the kids finish making one within a few minutes. This girl, though, keeps making hers more and more elaborate.

As she works, we sit at a table at the end of the shop and write clues on the cards. We decide to have the one Santa is going to hand her lead her to the elf working right here in the workshop. The one the elf hands her will take her to the stage, where the high school jazz band is playing, and right up to the saxophone player near the edge. He'll give her a card that leads her to the final place—the station where the city is handing out hot cocoa.

"Ava," the girl's mom says, "if you want to see Santa, you need to finish up within one minute."

"Ava!" Hammy whispers. I write her name on the cards and on the present. We hand one to the elf and then hurry over to Santa. As soon as the kid on his lap hops down, we slip in, hand him the card, point out the girl who is just coming out of the workshop, and ask if he'll give her the card before she leaves.

Then we get a good distance away to watch. The little girl, Ava, sits on Santa's lap, shows him the snowflake she made, and then talks animatedly. She's been rather reserved up to this point, and I love the excitement on her face as she tells him about the markers.

The band is nearing the end of *Deck the Halls*, so the second we see Santa hand the girl the card, we run to the stage. We ask the saxophone player to give the card to a little girl named Ava who comes up to him. Then we head to the hot cocoa station and hand them the gift with instructions to tell the girl it's from Santa.

We get hot cocoa ourselves and stand under a tree with the perfect view and wait, sipping our cocoa. For the first time, I notice that the night has gotten cold enough that we can see our breath. But there's a thrill running through me, so I don't care about the temperature.

Plus, Hammy is next to me, seeming every bit as elated as I am. Before long, we spot Ava, holding her snowflake in one hand and our cards in the other, her mom at her side. She walks up to the booth and says, "Hi, I'm Ava. This card told me to come here. Do you have something for me?"

They hand her the present and tell her it's from Santa. The little girl hugs it to her chest. Hammy slides his hand into mine, and we watch the girl's face fill with wonder.

"Are you going to open it?" her mom asks.

Ava shakes her head. "It's from Santa. It needs to go under the tree for Christmas morning."

Ava's mom looks around like she's trying to find who to thank. She has tears in her eyes. As a mom, I know the feeling of overwhelming gratitude that overcomes you when someone does something for your child that you couldn't do for them yourself. It makes me tear up a little, too.

I glance at Hammy. He's just as affected by the scene as I am. I definitely have some nagging worries about Hammy. But I've also got a great deal of respect for a man who'll get this choked up at a chance to provide Christmas for a little girl.

I lean my head against Hammy, and he lets go of my hand so he can put his arm around my shoulders while we spend the last few minutes before we meet up with the others to just take in the magic.

CHAPTER 5

A SPY, A SANDWICH, AND SOME SECRETS

Abraham

As long as there isn't an active mission that Charlie's needed for, we get together for lunch once a week. Today, it's at my desk in Sub-level One, and we're eating deli sandwiches and chips. Usually, Charlie tells me about her life. Things I imagine she'd tell her dad if he was alive. And then I tell her something about my life.

Today, though, she cuts straight to asking about mine. "So…" she says, dragging out the word as she picks up a potato chip, "I get the sense that you really like Reese's mom."

I knew the subject would arise. She's roommates with Reese, after all. I don't mind that she's asking—Annette hasn't left my mind since I met her. It's nice to actually talk about her.

"I do. I can tell she's worried I'm hiding something,

though—which I am—and that it'll start causing problems between us."

"So are you going to tell her?"

"I think so." I'm actually pretty nervous about it.

"Which part? Working for a secret intelligence agency or the part where you don't actually look like she thinks you do?"

I run my hands through my hair. "She needs to know both."

"Okay, so turn in the paperwork to get her approved to know the CSA stuff, and then tell her both."

I nod slowly and take a bite of my sandwich. Charlie's studying me. She can tell there's more to it than submitting a form and then telling Annette.

"What is it?" she asks.

"I want to be authentic with Annette. I just…don't know if I can."

Charlie is silent for a long moment as we each take another bite. Then she pushes her food aside and says, "For as long as I've known you, you've worn a disguise outside of work."

I nod.

"I don't know of a single other intelligence operative—ex or current—who wears a disguise for normal, everyday things. Do you feel like you have to, or are you doing it because you enjoy it?"

I think for a bit, trying to decide how to explain, then I shove my food aside, too. "My dad worked for the CIA as an operative."

Surprise crosses Charlie's face. It's not that I hide that fact. The topic just rarely comes up. "He loved that I was adventurous, and he wanted me to have an adventurous job when I grew up. Not that I needed to be an intelligence operative—he would've been just as thrilled if I became a helicopter pilot or a stunt coordinator. Maybe a racecar driver or a storm chaser.

"My mom, though, wanted me to nurture my artistic side. She was always worried about my dad and didn't want to worry about me, too."

"I bet she'd be so happy to know you're using your artistic side in your job now."

I smile. "I like to think she would." I take a deep breath. "When I was fourteen, there was an information breach. Some covert operatives were burned, including my dad, and a guy he'd tried to capture got that intel. My dad died because of it." I don't bring up that my best friend—Charlie's dad—also died because he'd been an operative, but I can tell that Charlie's thinking about it.

"So, maybe I've always worn it because I don't want someone I went after to come for me."

"You've been out of the field for a long time," Charlie says.

"I know. Many of the people who would've held a grudge probably aren't even alive anymore."

Charlie is silent for a moment. She can probably sense the "but" behind my words. I should tell her, but before I figure out if I can even find the words, she beats me to it. "But you still wear a disguise because you're afraid of people knowing the real you."

I chuckle and shake my head. "You've always been much too perceptive. Which is what makes you so good at your job."

Charlie grins.

"You know, maybe it isn't that I'm afraid of people

knowing the real me, but I'm afraid I don't know who the real me is anymore. I've been playing roles for too long. Maybe the real me got lost along the way."

Charlie tilts her head. "Is Abraham not your real name?"

I chuckle. "It's my real name." She knows it is.

"I've known you my entire life. It feels to me like you're the genuine Abraham."

"Well, I am *here*. I'm just not outside of these walls."

"So, you're not out of practice being you. You're just used to becoming Hammy when you leave."

True.

"I've also known you as Hammy for at least a year. I've seen how you are at Outside the Bubble and around town, and I'd say that Hammy and Abraham are practically identical. It's only the disguise that's different. If you drop that, you can live as the real, genuine, authentic you."

"You really think so?"

"I *know* so. Now go, get that form submitted so the Personnel Security Division can get Annette vetted before they leave for Christmas break, and then tell her already! It can be your Christmas gift to her. It can be your Christmas gift to *you*, too."

I'm smiling and feeling lighter already. And very much ready to not be alone anymore.

"You've got this," Charlie says, then grabs our mostly empty food cartons and heads toward the hall leading to the elevators. Then she turns and adds, "Oh, and Abe? Good luck, have fun, and don't die."

I chuckle and shake my head. She's right. I've got this.

CHAPTER 6

WRAP, WORRY, REPEAT

Annette

"*B*ut you like him, right?" Reese asks as she works alongside me at my kitchen table, wrapping presents, as we've been doing since I got home from work.

"I do!" I pick up Spark and she gives me kisses until I give her neck a good scratch. I hadn't wanted a dog. But then Dylan and Reese got me this sweetheart for my birthday this year to give me back "the spark" I'd lost—which is how she got her name—and I've been a devoted dog mom ever since.

I let out a breath. "It's just that I worry he's purposely hiding things. And I'm not talking about something like secretly needing to sleep with a fluffy eye mask, or loving polka music, or obsessing over reality dating shows. Those kinds of secrets are fine. I mean, I'm not in a hurry to tell him that I have an irrational fear of pigeons."

"*Pigeons?*"

"It's a thing. I'm talking about something big. Which is weird because he seems like the kind of guy who'd head back into the grocery store if he was putting his bags into his trunk and realized he didn't pay for a candy bar. So it doesn't make sense, but I don't know. It kind of freaks me out. Especially after—" Thankfully, I stop myself before finishing. I've been careful not to say anything bad to my kids about their dad because I don't want to sabotage their relationship with him.

But then Reese finishes for me. "—all of the stuff that Dad always hid?"

I look at her, shocked.

"Mom, I know. I mean, you're not the only one he hid stuff from." I must still be looking shocked because she adds, "What? Like I was supposed to believe he didn't show up to my school plays because of a 'work emergency' that magically happened every spring on the night of my performance?"

"I'm so sorry, honey," I say as I put my little pup back on the floor.

"Mom, we're talking about you and Hammy. Not me and Dad."

I take a deep breath and pull out the next present to be wrapped. "Okay, then, yes, because of that, it freaks me out. But the strange thing is, I'm not really freaked out while I'm with Hammy. I think because I have so much fun with him and enjoy his company. It's when we're *not* together that it gets in my head."

I turn the present over on the wrapping paper, measure how much I need, and then start to cut. "But I don't think that having Fun Annette 'come in from the cold'—don't ask—is a good enough reason by itself to continue dating him. I've never been interested in dating just for fun."

"And you don't think you like him enough for it to be more than 'just for fun'?"

I rub the side of my hand on my forehead before sighing. "No. I think I like him enough for it to be *everything*. That's what scares me."

Reese's face lights up at my admission. Before she gets too excited, I bring up my other worry. "Plus, there's our age gap to think about."

Reese nods. "Mackenzie thinks he's sixty-four. Twelve years is a pretty big gap."

"If I was younger, I might not think it was. But work is important to me."

Reese gives me a sly smile. "As it is to all driven workaholics."

I toss Reese a look. "It's not just me. I get the sense that Hammy's a 'driven workaholic,' too. But if he's sixty-four, he'll likely want to retire soon. I'm still fifteen years from considering that! If he retired and I kept working for that many years, we'd be living different lives with different goals. Maybe if we'd been married for decades already, our relationship could handle it. But for a new relationship? I can't see that working."

"So, are you thinking of ending things?"

"No. I don't know. Yes. Not because of the age gap —Hammy is a hidden gem and worth it, you know? But... after your dad," I say carefully, "I swore I'd never date someone who isn't truthful. If nothing else, I have to keep that promise to myself."

I give myself a nod. I have to stay strong. I can be strong in this.

My watch buzzes with a text, so I glance down and then look at Reese with wide eyes. "It's Hammy—he wants to come over. He really needs to talk to me about something." I respond with *Yes. I want to talk to you about something, also.* Tonight is as good as any to put the brakes on our relationship.

Worries start to worm their way in and I look at Reese, who's in the middle of wrapping a ribbon around a present. "Do you think he's going to tell me that he has another family somewhere?"

Then, I pace as panic sets in, and my brain runs through scenario after scenario of what he might tell me. "Maybe he was a rock star in his twenties and he's coming to tell me that they're getting the band back together and he's about to leave on an extended tour. Or he's an extreme prepper with an underground bunker packed with twenty years' worth of powdered potatoes and wants me to wait out the end of civilization with him.

"Oh! Maybe he's in witness protection because he was a mob boss who informed on his fellow mobsters so he could settle down after a life of crime." Why am I stressing over this crazy list of scenarios? If I'm going to end things, none of it matters.

Reese starts laughing. "Oh my gosh, Mom! I've never seen you like this before! Say what you want, but I think this means you *really* like him."

I stop pacing, let out a long, slow breath, and try to calm my heart rate, especially because Spark is getting rather concerned—and a little tired from pacing back and forth with me. "I know. I'm hopeless."

"Hopelessly in looooove," Reese sings like she's thirteen and she's teasing her brother about his first date.

I playfully swat at her with some ribbon. "It wouldn't

matter. I can't be with someone who is hiding big things. Now get. He's on his way over right now."

Reese walks to the entryway and grabs her coat from the rack and her keys from the side table. "Okay, but I want an update the minute Hammy leaves. I don't care how late it is."

"I am not calling you the minute he leaves."

"No, seriously. Treat it like when I was a teenager and going out—I had to tell you about every date the moment I got home, even if you were already asleep."

I put my hands on my hips. "I believe *I'm* the mom here."

Reese pauses with one hand on the doorknob. "And if you wait until morning to report in, I'm going assume he slept over," she says in that same singsong voice.

"Reese!"

"I'm out," she says as she opens the door. Just before she closes it behind her, she says, "Call me!"

I shake my head. *Kids.*

CHAPTER 7

CONFESSIONS OF A NOT-SO-BALDING MAN

Hammy / Abraham

Tonight is warmer than last night, which tells me the predicted snowfall is on its way. Flurries are already swirling as I walk to Annette's door and knock, a bag in my hand and my heart racing like a rookie operative on his first mission.

Spark barks just before Annette answers the door, her dog in one arm. She's wearing a cozy sweater and yoga pants, and she looks as beautiful and perfect as ever. "Come in." She leads us to her couch where we both sit and Spark nestles into her side.

I like this room. The couch faces a fireplace with two narrow but tall windows flanking the sides of it, and Christmas decorations are all around. Her tree has a mix of traditional ornaments and ones likely made by her kids when they were young. Pictures of Dylan and Reese as both children and adults sit on the mantle. A bigger, framed family picture that includes her daughter-in-law and granddaughter adorns one wall, and a collage of her kids and her dog are on another. It's clear that family is important to her by this room alone.

I take a deep breath, then decide to just get right to it and say, "There's something I haven't told you about me that I really want you to know," at the same time she says, "Okay, I have to say this before I chicken out."

Then, at least partially hearing what I said, she asks, "Wait, what?"

"You can go first."

Annette pauses, holding her breath, before she shakes her head. "You can."

She is so beautiful. The look on her face is one of wariness, though, and it might've made me hold back if I didn't want so badly for her to know everything. "I have things about me I want to tell you, and I now have permission to do so." That sentence didn't lessen the wary look on her face at all. "I told you that I work at a business solutions company. Lancaster Business Solutions, specifically."

She nods as she absently pets Spark.

"That's our cover name."

"Cover name?" she asks, her hand freezing mid-pet.

"I actually work for the Clandestine Services Agency. It's a top-secret government intelligence agency." I search her expression, which I'm pretty adept at doing, yet I can't guess what she's thinking.

Then she laughs. It's not a happy laugh, though, and it makes her stand and walk a few steps away, Spark following her, before she turns back to say, "Now, see? This is why we need to talk. I need to be able to trust what you tell me."

"I know," I say, pleading with my eyes for her to come back. She must sense my earnestness in wanting her to know what I'm about to say because she sits back down, turned toward me. "After how much we've joked about me being a spy, I worried it wouldn't sound believable. So I brought this." I pull my work lanyard and badge from my bag and hand it to her.

She takes it in both hands and inspects it. "Huh. This looks pretty legit." She turns the badge over, runs a finger across my name, the CSA's emblem, the hologram, and the watermark, touches corners worn from years of use, and the fraying part of the lanyard that rubs against my desk when I lean in. Spark climbs over her to check it out, too.

I wait until her eyes meet mine before I say, "This isn't one we'd use in the field, of course. It's strictly for in-house purposes—accessing locked areas and the like."

I pull out my business phone. "This is the phone I answered the day we tubed down Doomslide Summit. It's for work, and it's encrypted." I tap on the screen until I've opened my email from the Personnel Security Division. "I have permission to show you this. It's the form I submitted to let them know I'm interested in pursuing a relationship with you."

Then I tap on the reply. "And here's their response, saying that you've been vetted and cleared to be read in on my title, basic responsibilities, the name of the agency, and any other information necessary that does not require a security clearance."

I hand the phone to her, and she looks at it, her eyes moving quickly enough that she's probably only catching a few words here and there as her mind whirls. "They had to clear me before you told me?"

I nod, and she keeps staring at it. Eventually, she hands the phone back. "Wow. 'Secret agency' was not one of my guesses. You said you work in graphic design?"

"Well," I shrug, "graphic design of the face. Sometimes the whole body."

"This is huge. Were you always in that department?"

I can't even guess how she feels about any of this, though I am trying. "No. I spent many years as an intelligence operative. I only moved to my current department when I retired from field work."

"You were *a spy*?"

I hide my flinch—years of practice—and say, "Yes. Basically a spy."

She studies me. "So, did you really have 'Covert infiltration' training?"

"Yes."

"You didn't tell me all this because I said I needed excitement in my life, right?"

I chuckle. "I don't know about you, but I think we've had plenty of excitement since we met, even without this."

I know she agrees because, for the first time tonight, a bit of a smile crosses her face. She's quiet again then shakes her head. "This explains a lot. But not why several of the Lancasters didn't seem to recognize you."

"Yeah," I say, grimacing, "my occupation isn't the only thing I need to tell you about." She's studying me again, all her focus on my face. "I think it'll be easier to show you."

I pull from my bag the case that stores my facial appliances. Then, one at a time, I peel off the pieces affixed to my face that make me look a little older, a little more wrinkled, my eyebrows a bit bushier, and place them in the case. Annette watches in disbelief. I remove the cap and wig that make my hair appear more balding and whiter. My hair is actually a dark gray with light gray at the temples. I put it all in my bag and run my hands through my hair because I know how it probably looks.

Annette gapes at me, more shocked than when I told her who I work for. I get it—it's disconcerting to see someone's appearance change right before your eyes. "So, yeah," I say. "This is me."

"Why? Why are you wearing a disguise? Do you wear it everywhere? I don't understand."

"I don't wear it to work—only around town. Most of the Lancasters hadn't seen me wearing it until that day at the park. As for the reason why…" I take a deep breath because this requires even more vulnerability than taking the disguise off did. "Until recently, I thought I was being smart and safe. My dad was killed by someone he'd tried to capture as an intelligence operative. He'd been recognized as he came out of a movie theater."

"Oh, Hammy. I'm so sorry."

"It was almost forty years ago. I'm okay. I realized that somewhere along the way, though, I became accustomed to hiding behind a disguise. To hiding who I really am."

The expression on her face is changing, so I push forward. "And then you came along. I've never known anyone as incredible as you. I've never been captivated the way you've captivated me. I've never wanted someone to see the real me before you came along.

"I've spent my life hiding, Annette, and I don't want to hide from you. I want you to see… Me. The real me."

CHAPTER 8

THE SPY WHO CAME IN FROM THE COLD...
WITH COOKIES

Annette

"So," I say, "instead of hiding things from me, you're hiding things from everyone else and revealing them only to me."

He grimaces. "It's bad. I'm so sorry."

"No, oddly, it feels very different from the other way around."

All of this has completely blown my mind. When I'd been guessing what Hammy might tell me, I'd guessed utterly outlandish things. But this is every bit as big as my guesses were.

I know I'm in a bit of shock. But also, there's a happiness coursing through me now. I love knowing this about Hammy. I love that I'm important enough to him that he's willing to share this when he's kept it secret for so many years.

"So," I ask, needing to know, "you aren't going to retire

anytime soon, are you?"

"Heavens, no! I love my job way too much. They'd have to kick me out and revoke my security clearance to get me to stop coming." He lifts one shoulder in a shrug. "Plus, I started working at the CSA when it first became an agency. There are two other guys—one in logistics and one in cover and legend development who still work there. I need to outlast them both. Wait. Were you hoping I would?"

I shake my head. "I really wasn't." His answer makes my soul sing. Finding out that we're on the same page is a glorious feeling.

"I don't have to keep wearing the disguise."

I try to hold back a smile. "So you're suddenly going to start looking a decade younger?"

Hammy laughs.

"Do you want to stop?" I ask him. "Because I'll love you whether you look like you or like my mailman who just retired."

"You love me?" The look on Hammy's face is both hopeful and measured.

I smile. "I think maybe I do."

"And you really don't care how old I look?"

"I really don't."

He nods slowly. "Okay. I think I'm ready to be myself. I want to be the genuine article."

"You know, you could slowly use less and less of your disguise."

He smiles. "I could tell people that being around you makes me younger."

I laugh. "I know being around you makes me feel younger."

"We've had a lot of fun together."

"Mmm," I agree. "You told me that you aren't *always* out having fun, though. Sometimes you stay in for cocoa cookie nights. That sounds pretty wonderful tonight."

Hammy pulls a plastic container from his bag. "I just happen to have baked hot cocoa cookies tonight. I gave you the store-bought kind before, but I figured the real thing might help ease the shock of all I've told you. Plus, making them gave me time to figure out how I would tell you."

"You, Hammy, are a gem."

I stand, which of course makes Spark hop off the couch and follow me as I lower the lights and turn on some soft music. Then I switch on the Christmas tree lights. Snow is silently falling in big, chunky flakes, shining brightly in the moonlight through the windows. I go over to the fireplace, flip the switch to light it, and when I turn back, Hammy is standing, and we move in close together.

He reaches up to pull an errant ribbon scrap from my messy bun, and the touch sends a thrill through me. Then his eyes meet mine. "You are an incredible woman, Annette. Did you know that? I laid a lot on you tonight. It'd be reasonable for you to tell me to go away and then bury yourself under a pile of blankets."

I place my hands on his chest and then slide them up to interlock my fingers behind his neck. "If it was anyone other than you, maybe I would. But you are pretty incredible yourself."

He's gazing at me like I'm the most wondrous thing he's ever seen. Like I'm the magic of Christmas from every year of his life wrapped up in one package. Music is playing, Spark is at my feet, the fire is crackling, the snow is falling, the lights are twinkling, and I can't imagine a more perfect moment.

"I love you, Annette."

And, it just became more perfect. His words send a thrill through my entire body. He tips his head down as I tip mine up and he kisses me. His lips are soft against mine, and I moan at their touch. He kisses me like I am cherished. Like I am someone to protect at all costs. Like I am special. Vitally important. Loved. Like I am everything.

I pull him as close to me as I can and he wraps his arms around me, holding me as much as I'm holding him. He's made me feel happy, hopeful, alive, excited, safe, and loved when I wasn't sure I could ever feel loved again. I want to hold onto this man forever.

Eventually, we move to the couch where I snuggle into him and Spark snuggles into my other side. I lean against Hammy's chest, soaking in the sound of his heart and the feel of his arm around me as we watch the snow fall and the fire burn.

Then I ask, "So is that why you never married? Because you were a spy and it was too dangerous?"

"That," he says, "and because my schedule was never predictable. I sometimes spent weeks out of town. I didn't think it was possible to have the life of a spy and a real relationship." He pauses a moment, then adds, "That's a lie, because my best friend, Rick, met a woman who was also a spy, got married, had six kids, and that worked out great. But they had an epic kind of love—not the kind normal people have."

I tilt my head to look at him. "You don't think you can have an epic kind of love? Because from what I know of you…"

He smiles. "Well, I never thought I could until I met you."

"Wow. That's a really great answer. You get bonus points for that one." I feel his rumbling chuckle as much as I hear it.

Then I sit up. "Oh! This is all top secret! Reese was here when I got your text—she knows you came to tell me something and she'll ask about it. What do I tell her?"

"If it's okay with you, I'd rather you not mention the CSA, since she hasn't been cleared. As far as everyone knows, I work at Lancaster Business Solutions. That's what it says on our building. It's what my business cards say."

I nod. "Okay, that's easy." I pause. "But then what do I tell her you told me? Oh! We could say that you testified against a mob boss. He was convicted, but you knew he could still send someone after you, so you had to have a disguise. But the mob boss died, so you no longer have to hide."

Now Hammy is the one trying to suppress a smile. "Is that what you guessed I was going to tell you?"

"Well, it's *one* of the things I kind of guessed. You don't want to know the other ones."

He chuckles.

"I need to call Reese tonight and tell her the story before she gets crazy ideas." We each take one of Hammy's hot cocoa cookies from the container and take a bite. I moan as I chew. "I thought the ones you got from the bakery were delicious, but *these*." I take another bite and moan again. "These are to die for."

Hammy's smile widens.

When I finish my first cookie—I plan to eat several—I say, "I noticed the name on your CSA badge is *Abraham*. Would you like me to call you Abraham or Hammy?"

He shrugs. "I have a fondness for both. Which do you prefer?"

"Well, you see, I developed a huge fondness for the name *Hammy* around the time I got tangled in Christmas lights with a stranger." I smile. "And I think I always will."

EPILOGUE

OPERATION: NEWLYWED

Hammy
One year later

"**I** think everything is ready!" Annette says as she opens the oven.

"Here, I've got this," I say, making sure not to step on Spark as I take the honey-glazed ham out of the oven. Annette pulls out the dish of scalloped potatoes, and I take out the roasted Brussels sprouts. Then Annette puts in the apple crisp so it'll be cooked and slightly cooled by the time we eat it.

We've all been working together in the kitchen to prepare the meal—Annette and I, along with Reese and Dylan, Dylan's wife, Jenna, their toddler daughter, Jovie, and their newborn son, Dax.

Well, technically Dax hasn't been helping unless you count how great he is at "keeping spirits bright." He's only a few weeks old, and he's the cutest thing I've ever seen. This is, hands-down, the best Christmas Eve I've ever had.

I put my arms around Annette, drop her into a dip, and give her a kiss. I mean for it to be a peck, but Annette presses her lips into mine like she wants us to stay like this forever, and it's all I can do to lift her upright and pull away after a couple of seconds.

"Get a room!" Jovie says in her cute little I-recently-learned-how-to-talk voice. Then she starts laughing uncontrollably, her little hands on her belly. Dylan, who's setting the table, is trying to look like he's innocent and didn't just whisper to Jovie to say that.

Reese turns from where she's putting buttery rolls into a basket at the counter and points at her brother. "You guys can't complain—you're the ones who gave her the 'Kiss the Christmas Bride' apron."

Annette and I got married two days ago, on the one-year anniversary of her seeing the real me. We had the ceremony and celebration at a rustic barn here in Cipher Springs. Everything was decorated in white, silver, and ice blue, with twinkling lights and candle-lit lanterns. We even had several cozy fires burning in outdoor pits where guests could gather with blankets and mugs of hot cocoa and cider as they socialized.

Sure, a snowstorm the morning of the wedding threatened to close roads, one of the songs for the dancing portion of the evening (*The Chicken Dance*) accidentally played as the bridesmaids and groomsmen walked down the aisle, and Jovie decided she was done being the flower girl halfway through sprinkling flower petals and chucked the basket, hitting a guest, but it made a perfect day all the more memorable. Everyone we love celebrated with us. Annette was a vision, and I'll forever keep in memory the image of her across from me as we said our vows.

Reese, Dylan, Jenna, and the kids stayed here for the wedding and are staying through Christmas. Having everyone under one roof has been unlike anything I've experienced, and my life feels infinitely richer having experienced it now.

And the day after Christmas, we'll be leaving on our honeymoon for a tropical adventure in French Polynesia.

We're moving the serving platters to the table as Jenna comes in, holding the freshly-changed and awake little bundle of joy. "I think Dax can tell it's dinnertime because he's awake and wanting attention."

"Of course he is," I say. "How about I hold him while you eat?" Jenna looks like she's starving and truth be told, I've been snitching enough bites as we've been cooking that I have no problem waiting. Especially if it means holding Dax.

Jenna looks at the baby in her arms. "Hey, sweetie. Do you want Grandpa to hold you?"

Grandpa. I'm beaming. I know I'm beaming. Being given that title is the coolest thing in the world.

She places him into my arms, and I cradle him so gently. Annette comes up to my side and we soak in how amazing this tiny person is and how great it is to be together. After we say grace and everyone starts dishing up and eating, I make faces and funny sounds at the little guy and let him wrap his hand around my finger.

"You know," I say, "I saw a plaque once that said something along the lines of 'If I'd known that grandkids would be so much fun, I'd have had them first.' Not that I've experienced it both ways, but I have to say this is a pretty great way to go about it."

I meet Annette's eyes and we both smile. I know she's

enjoying this day as much as I am. I'm going to snapshot today and keep it forever in memory, too.

I love my life. I wish I had found Annette when I was a young intelligence operative in the field and could tell myself a relationship was possible. My life would've been so different if she'd been in it all this time.

Although, maybe I needed to go through everything I did to become the right person for her. So I'll just be grateful that I have her in my life now and going forward. Because something tells me I'll be snapshotting in memory every day from here on out.

AUTHOR'S NOTE:

I hope you have enjoyed reading Annette's and Hammy's story! Hammy is a recurring side character in my Romancing the Spy romcom series, where each Lancaster sibling will get a book telling their love story. Hammy is a character I've loved from the moment he first stepped onto the page, and I've been so excited to share with you his story of falling in love with Annette.

If you enjoyed this novella, I think you'll love the Romancing the Spy series! They're longer books and are filled with humor, adventure, fun, and all the feels of a new couple falling in love. If you haven't read them already, I hope you give them a try and fall in love with the Lancaster family.

And make sure you continue reading to get the recipe for Hammy's Hot Cocoa Cookies!

–Meg

READ THE ROMANCING THE SPY SERIES

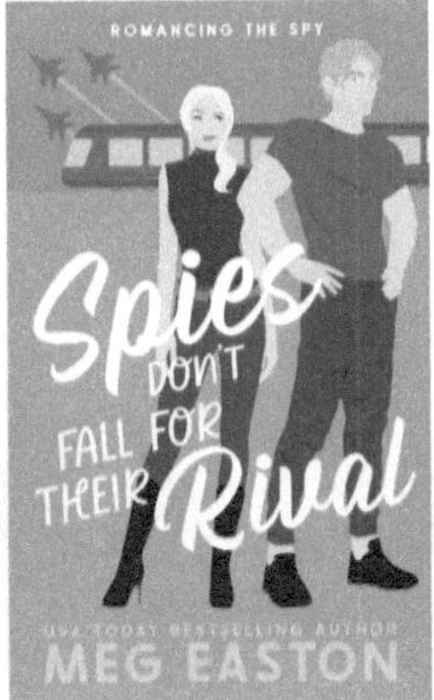

Spies Don't Fall for Their Asset
(Mackenzie's and Jace's story)

Spies Don't Fall for Their Rival
(Ledger's and Zoe's story)

Spies Don't Fall for Their Neighbor
(Charlie's and Owen's story)

*If you're not a fan of spice, just skip the chipotle/cayenne in both the dough and the sugar mixture.

Cookie dough:

- 1 cup (2 sticks) room temperature butter
- 1 ½ cup sugar
- 2 large eggs
- 1 tsp. vanilla
- 2 ¼ cups all-purpose flour or 1:1 gluten-free flour
- ½ cup cocoa powder
- 2 tsp. cream of tartar
- 1 tsp. baking soda

- ¼ tsp. salt
- ¼ tsp. ground chipotle powder OR red cayenne
  pepper

Sugar mixture:

- ¼ c. sugar
- ¼ tsp. ground chipotle powder OR red cayenne
  pepper
- 1 tsp. cinnamon

Preheat oven to 400°F

To make the dough: cream together butter and sugar until fluffy. Add eggs and vanilla and beat. Sift together all dry ingredients, then mix while gradually adding to the dough.

To make sugar mixture: combine all three ingredients.

Using a cookie scoop or spoon, form balls of dough and roll in the sugar mixture. Bake 3 inches apart on a parchment-lined baking sheet for 10 minutes. Let cookies cool on sheet for 3 minutes before transferring them to a wire rack. Makes about 4 dozen cookies.

If you enjoyed *Holiday Lights and Cocoa Cookie Nights*, jingle all the way through the festive season with ELEVEN more Christmas novellas that are little bites of sweet and swoony delight. These heartwarming and feel-good romances feature second chances, enemies turned lovers, fake dating adventures, and more, all wrapped up in the cozy merriment of the holidays. Plus, there's a cookie recipe in each book! Read them all.

ABOUT MEG EASTON

Meg Easton is the *USA Today* bestselling author of contemporary romances and romantic comedies with fun, memorable, swoon-worthy characters, and settings you'll want to pack up and move to. She lives at the foot of a mountain with her name on it (or at least one letter of her name) in Utah. She loves gardening, bike riding, baking, swimming before the sun rises, and spending time with her husband and three kids.

She can be found online at www.megeaston.com

Sign up to receive her newsletter and stay up to date with new releases, get exclusive bonus content, and more.

If you liked this book please leave a review. Your review can help other readers find books they might fall in love with.

youtube.com/@megeastonauthor
bookbub.com/authors/meg-easton
instagram.com/megeaston_author
facebook.com/MegEastonBooks
tiktok.com/@megeaston_author